To Elijah.
May all your Christmas
wishes come true!

Love...................................

A gift from Reynolds PTA

Elijah is ⇒**excited**⇐
Christmastime is here!

He says, "I wish for lots and lots
of fluffy snow this year!"

Elijah writes to Santa.
The letter takes him ages.

"Perhaps I've wished for way too much?"
(There are over 50 pages!)

Dear Santa,

Elijah decorates the tree
with twinkly lights that glow.

Elijah is up on stage.
He's in the Christmas play.

He wished to make
his family proud,
and have the greatest day!

The kitchen's very busy.
Elijah can smell baking.

"I wish that I could eat that bowl of cookie dough Dad's making."

He runs downstairs to find a pile of presents beneath the tree.

This sweater's really **itchy**.
He tries to grin and bear it.
Elijah really wishes that
he didn't have to wear it!

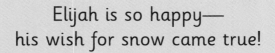

Elijah is so happy—
his wish for snow came true!

He's off to build a snowman now.
Perhaps he will build two!

Elijah is out sledding.
"I wish I could *speed* up!"

ELIJAH

His wish comes true,
his sled is *fast*
when powered by a pup!

zZz zZz zZz zZz

zzzzzZZZZzzzzzzZZZ

It's after Christmas dinner,
and everyone is snoring.
Elijah says to his best friend,
"I wish it was less **BORING!**"

Mom turns to Elijah,
"Did your **BIGGEST** wish come true?"
"Oh yes," he smiles,
"that wish was being..."

"...here with **all** of you!"

Do you wish for fun with friends,
or a family trip that never ends?
Whatever it is that you hold dear,
keep your Christmas wishes here!

I wish...

Published by Put Me In The Story,
a publication of Sourcebooks, Inc.
P.O. Box 4410, Naperville, Illinois 60567-4410
(630) 961-3900
Fax: (630) 961-2168
www.putmeinthestory.com

Date of Production: August 2018
Run Number: HTW_PO201829
Printed and bound in China (GD)
10 9 8 7 6 5 4 3 2 1

put **me**
in the **story**®

Bestselling books starring your child!
www.putmeinthestory.com

SANTA
STOP
HERE!